POLITICAL PRISONERS

Incarceration Issues:
Punishment, Reform, and Rehabilitation

TITLE LIST

POLITICAL PRISONERS

by Roger Smith

$$V = x(G)^0$$

Mason Crest Publishers
Philadelphia

Mason Crest Publishers Inc.
370 Reed Road
Broomall, Pennsylvania 19008
(866) MCP-BOOK (toll free)

First printing
1 2 3 4 5 6 7 8 9 10

Library of Congress Cataloging-in-Publication Data

Smith, Roger, 1959 Aug. 15–
  Political prisoners / by Roger Smith.
     p. cm. — (Incarceration issues)
  Includes bibliographical references and index.
  ISBN 1-59084-987-6   ISBN 1-59084-984-1 (series)
  ISBN 978-1-59084-987-6   ISBN 978-1-59084-984-2 (series)

  1. Political prisoners—Juvenile literature. I. Title. II. Series.
  HV8665.S63 2007
  365'.45—dc22
                        2006001488

Interior design by MK Bassett-Harvey.
Interiors produced by Harding House Publishing Service, Inc.
www.hardinghousepages.com

Cover design by Peter Spires Culotta.

Printed in India by Quadra Press.

Contents

INTRODUCTION

by Larry E. Sullivan, Ph.D.

Prisons will be with us as long as we have social enemies. We will punish them for acts that we consider criminal, and we will confine them in institutions.

Prisons have a long history, one that fits very nicely in the religious context of sin, evil, guilt, and expiation. In fact, the motto of one of the first prison reform organizations was "Sin no more." Placing offenders in prison was, for most of the history of the prison, a ritual for redemption through incarceration; hence the language of punishment takes on a very theological cast. The word "penitentiary" itself comes from the religious concept of penance. When we discuss prisons, we are dealing not only with the law but with very strong emotions and reactions to acts that range from minor or misdemeanor crimes to major felonies like murder and rape.

Prisons also reflect the level of the civilizing process through which a culture travels, and it tells us much about how we treat our fellow human beings. The great nineteenth-century Russian author Fyodor Dostoyevsky, who was a political prisoner, remarked, "The degree of civilization in a society can be measured by observing its prisoners." Similarly, Winston Churchill, the great British prime minister during World War II, said that the "treatment of crime and criminals is one of the most unfailing tests of civilization of any country."

Since the very beginnings of the American Republic, we have attempted to improve and reform the way we imprison criminals. For much of the history of the American prison, we tried to rehabilitate or modify the criminal behavior of offenders through a variety of treatment programs. In the last quarter of the twentieth century, politicians and citizens alike realized that this attempt had failed, and we began passing stricter laws, imprisoning people for longer terms and building more prisons. This movement has taken a great toll on society. Approximately two million people are behind bars today. This movement has led to the

overcrowding of prisons, worse living conditions, fewer educational programs, and severe budgetary problems. There is also a significant social cost, since imprisonment splits families and contributes to a cycle of crime, violence, drug addiction, and poverty.

All these are reasons why this series on incarceration issues is extremely important for understanding the history and culture of the United States. Readers will learn all facets of punishment: its history; the attempts to rehabilitate offenders; the increasing number of women and juveniles in prison; the inequality of sentencing among the races; attempts to find alternatives to incarceration; the high cost, both economically and morally, of imprisonment; and other equally important issues. These books teach us the importance of understanding that the prison system affects more people in the United States than any institution, other than our schools.

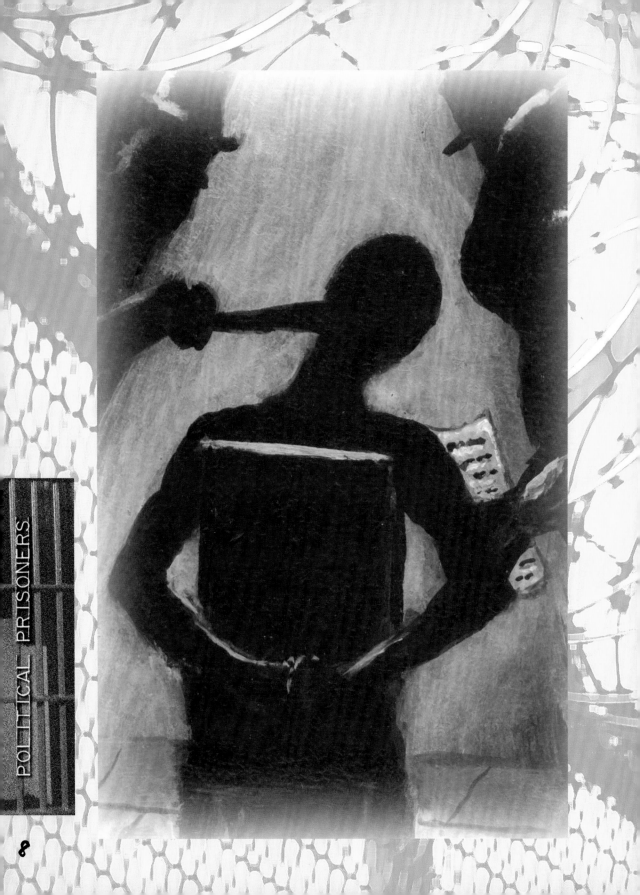

POLITICAL PRISONERS

CHAPTER 1.

POLITICAL IMPRISONMENT

"Now I swing between the deepest resentment and the sincere wish to feel no more hatred. Hatred eats you up. . . . Hatred will never enable me to make up for the lost years."
—Malika Oufkir

Malika Oufkir has experienced things few people in twenty-first-century North America could even imagine. For a few years, she lived a fairy tale, and then for two decades, her life was a nightmare. She, her five siblings, and her mother were political prisoners held under unbearable conditions as punishment for her father's crime.

Malika, whose name means "Princess" in Arabic, was born in 1953 in the Kingdom of Morocco. Her mother loved movies, shopping, horse riding, and Elvis Presley; her father was head of the Moroccan police and close to the king. When Malika was five years old, King Muhammad V saw her playing with his daughter. The king told Malika's parents, "I wish to adopt your daughter"; he wanted her to be a playmate for his child. Immediately, she moved into the palace. She had the best of everything—education, toys, and royal treatment—yet she could not leave the palace.

When she was sixteen, Malika rebelled against the limitations of living in the royal court, and the king allowed her to leave the palace. For the next few years, she lived a dream, as her parents were wealthy and famous, and she was young and beautiful. She traveled to Paris and the United States, where famous politicians and movie stars paid attention to her. She dreamed of making movies in Hollywood, and she might have done so if cruel fate had not intervened.

On August 16, 1972, Malika was relaxing with friends in her house in Casablanca when she switched on the television; in a single moment, her life changed forever. The news announcer said an unsuccessful *coup* had taken place against the king, led by General Oufkir—Malika's father. Shortly after, her father called Malika, telling her that he was proud of her and loved her. The next day, Malika was staring at her father's bullet-ridden body, and almost at once, the king took her, her siblings, and her mother into custody.

On Christmas Eve of that year, a big car with blacked-out windows, escorted by armed police, drove the survivors of the Oufkir family to a secret desert prison. Malika writes: "This was a country where they locked up young children for their father's crimes. We were entering the world of insanity." At age nineteen, Malika was the oldest child; her youngest brother, Abdellatif, was only three years old.

From 1973 to 1977, the Moroccan government imprisoned the Oufkirs in a ruined fortress named Tamattaght. The summer heat was stifling, and the winter cold biting. Huge rats crawled into the prison, where the mother and children beat them off with sticks. "I thought there were

Malika grew up in Morocco's royal palace.

Morocco's King Hassan

limits to human suffering," Malika Oufkir writes, but at their next place of imprisonment, "I was to discover there were none."

For ten years, King Hassan II held the Oufkirs at Bir-Jdid Prison, near Casablanca, each in solitary confinement. The children had smuggled pigeons from Tamattaght to Bir-Jdid, as these pets helped them to feel less lonely. The guards at Bir-Jdid discovered the pigeons and made a cruel game of killing them in front of the children. Little Abdellatif, who had just turned eight, tried unsuccessfully to kill himself.

The family lived in wretched conditions: wounds, illnesses, improper sanitation, lack of privacy, cockroaches, mosquitoes, mice, and rats plagued them. On top of that, the guards practically starved them to death. "Hunger humiliates, hunger debases," Malika writes. "Hunger turns you into a monster. We were always hungry."

For almost a decade, the mother and children fought against insanity. Malika made up stories they passed secretly from cell to cell as a way of remembering their humanity and relieving the maddening boredom of solitary confinement. Finally, they were all at their wits' end. The mother and oldest brother attempted suicide, but they were too weak to succeed. At that point, the Oufkirs decided their only hope of survival was escape.

Using a spoon, a knife handle, the lid of a sardine tin, and an iron bar from one of the beds, they began to tunnel between their cells and under the walls of their prison. Each morning, they carefully replaced the stones atop their tunnel so guards would not notice. On April 19, 1987, Malika and three of her siblings shoved their bodies through the narrow tunnel, under the walls, and up into the dark desert night—they were free!

Although they had escaped, the four Oufkir siblings had to endure almost a week of terrifying, frustrating efforts to make contact with people who could help them reach *asylum*. They attempted to contact family members, former friends, and foreign embassies, but their efforts to find refuge failed repeatedly; when they most desperately needed help, it seemed no one would assist them.

The Oufkirs' salvation came about due to an official visit to Morocco by French president Francois Mitterrand. The four siblings contacted a member of the president's party, and President Mitterrand sent them a

message: "You should be very proud of yourselves because while there are millions of children who are persecuted, massacred and imprisoned in the world, you will be remembered as the only ones who did not give up and continued to fight to the end."

France publicized the Oufkirs' plight, and though the Moroccan police soon found them, King Hassan II did not dare send them back to prison while the world was watching. He released their mother and the other two siblings, and they all lived for the next five years in what Malika calls "a strange kind of freedom," officially free to go anywhere in Morocco yet continually followed by police, their phones tapped, their friends interrogated, and every step of their lives under surveillance. Finally, as the twentieth century neared its end, several of the Oufkir children managed to marry citizens of other countries and obtain legal emigration for the other family members out of Morocco. They were genuinely free at last, but the scars of decades in prison would continue to haunt them.

Malika is now married to a Frenchman named Eric and lives in Paris. According to the U.S. Department of State Reports on Human Rights Practices, in Morocco, in 2004, "Although progress continued in some areas, the human rights record remained poor in other areas. . . . The Constitution does not prohibit *arbitrary* arrest or detention, and police continued to use these practices."

POLITICAL IMPRISONMENT DEFINED

As defined by the *Oxford History of the Prison*, a political prisoner is "someone who is incarcerated for his or her beliefs." According to Wikipedia, the collaborative online encyclopedia, "A political prisoner is anyone held in prison or otherwise detained, perhaps under house arrest, because their ideas either challenge or pose a real or potential threat to the state. In many cases, a veneer of legality is used to disguise the fact that someone is a political prisoner."

POLITICAL PRISONERS HALL OF FAME

In the seventeenth, eighteenth, and nineteenth centuries, a number of famous figures served time in prison as political prisoners. In sixteenth-century England, John Bunyan, the Baptist author of the classic *Pilgrim's Progress,* served time in prison for his religious beliefs, as did the founder of the Pennsylvania colony, William Penn. In France, the philosopher Voltaire was jailed twice for speaking against the government. The famous American writer Henry David Thoreau spent two nights in Concord jail in July of 1846, for refusing to pay taxes that helped fund the Mexican-American War. He wrote his famous essay "Resistance to Civil Government" because of this experience. That essay has influenced generations of political activists, although Thoreau's jail experience was very brief and painless compared to the experiences of countless other political prisoners.

The term political prisoner is sometimes confused with another expression, prisoner of conscience, but the two expressions are not identical. A political prisoner is someone imprisoned primarily because of his or her beliefs, but a political prisoner could also have engaged in violent acts. Contrasting with this, a prisoner of conscience is in prison because of his or her beliefs but who has *not* engaged in any form of violence.

To illustrate the difference, Nelson Mandela became one of history's most famous political prisoners when the South African government incarcerated him for opposing the practice of **apartheid**. However, Amnesty International refused to categorize Mandela as a prisoner of conscience, because his companions sometimes used violence in their struggle for racial justice. Dr. Martin Luther King, who steadfastly opposed violence in his fight for racial equality in the United States, was

BEFORE HIS IMPRISONMENT, EUGENE DEBS GAVE THIS SPEECH IN CANTON, OHIO, ON JUNE 16, 1918:

To speak for labor; to plead the cause of the men and women and children who toil; to serve the working class, has always been to me a high privilege; a duty of love. . . . I realize that, in speaking to you this afternoon, there are certain limitations placed upon the right of free speech. I must be exceedingly careful, prudent, as to what I say, and even more careful and prudent as to how I say it. I may not be able to say all I think; but I am not going to say anything that I do not think. I would rather a thousand times be a free soul in jail than to be a sycophant and coward in the streets.

Eugene Debs delivering his speech at Canton, Ohio

both a political prisoner and a prisoner of conscience when incarcerated in the Birmingham, Alabama, jail.

Whether someone is a "political prisoner" depends on one's perspective. In the twenty-first century, most national governments agree that political imprisonment is immoral; likewise, most governments deny holding political prisoners.

THE CENTURY OF POLITICAL IMPRISONMENT—THE 1900S

During World War I and the decade that followed, the United States and Great Britain imprisoned a number of political prisoners, namely "radicals" and those opposed to the war. Eugene Debs was a famous political prisoner of that time. While in prison, he received almost a million votes as the presidential nominee of the Socialist Party.

Sentencing Debs to jail, U.S. Supreme Court justice Oliver Wendell Holmes stated: "When a nation is at war, many things that might be said in times of peace . . . will not be endured so long as men fight and no court could regard them as protected by any constitutional right." In other words, the circumstances of war might override the ordinary constitutional rights of U.S. citizens. This principle is significant as it affects the likelihood of political imprisonment during war, and it is still controversial today in its expression within the Patriot Act.

At the end of World War I, the Bolsheviks overthrew the Russian monarchy, ushering in almost a century of communism in Eastern Europe. In the United States, national officials responded to the "Red Scare" by imprisoning communist party members and other radicals. In 1919 and 1920, the U.S. government arrested more than 3,000 people for their communist or other "radical" tendencies.

In the meantime, the Bolsheviks in Russia were busy imprisoning or executing peasants, soldiers, and politicians en masse, finishing off the opposition to their recent revolution. In 1928, Joseph Stalin took over leadership of the Russian Communist Party and increased the scope of

Oliver Wendell Holmes, often considered one of America's greatest legal minds, believed that constitutional rights no longer exist during times of war.

political persecution and imprisonment. By 1938, the Russian government had incarcerated an estimated seven million people, or one of every fifteen Russian citizens.

Stalin's massive political imprisonment was about to be overshadowed by even greater horrors in Germany. The ***pogram*** was the attempt by Adolf Hitler and the Nazi Party in Germany, before and during World War II, to exterminate all persons deemed "undesirable" by the party.

No one is sure of the exact numbers, but historians estimate that the Nazis killed between ten and fourteen million people in what has become known as the Holocaust. The death camps were the primary tools for this slaughter; these were massive facilities imprisoning men, women, and children for the purposes of slave labor or death in gas chambers. The death camps were also factories, where Nazis processed the corpses of their victims to create products for the war effort. In the entirety of human history, the Holocaust ranks as one of the very worst tragedies.

After the war, Russia continued to send men, women, and children to the Gulag, a network of forced labor camps in Siberia, used mostly for political prisoners who opposed the Soviet state. More than a million people died in these camps, where the government forced them to do harsh labor logging or mining, and kept them underfed and poorly sheltered. Eighty percent of prisoners died during their first months in the Gulag.

Political historians call the closing years of the twentieth century "the human rights era." Trials of the Nazi death camp guards alerted the world to the importance of rights for political prisoners. In 1948, the United Nations adopted the Universal Declaration of Human Rights: only three countries—the Soviet Union, South Africa, and Saudi Arabia—failed to support the declaration. By the end of the twentieth century, apartheid had ended in South Africa, along with the massive incarceration of political opponents to that system of segregation. Communism collapsed in Eastern Europe, ending mass incarceration of political prisoners in the former Soviet Union.

As a new millennium begins, political imprisonment is far from finished. According to the 2005 Freedom House report *Freedom in the World*, Burma, Cuba, Libya, North Korea, Saudi Arabia, Sudan, Syria, and Turkmenistan are among the nations most notorious for political imprisonment. These are by no means the only offenders. According to the report, "Massive human rights violations take part in nearly every part of the world." In the following pages, we meet some of the important people who have served time as political prisoners in history, and some of the brave women and men who continue to suffer imprisonment for their beliefs.

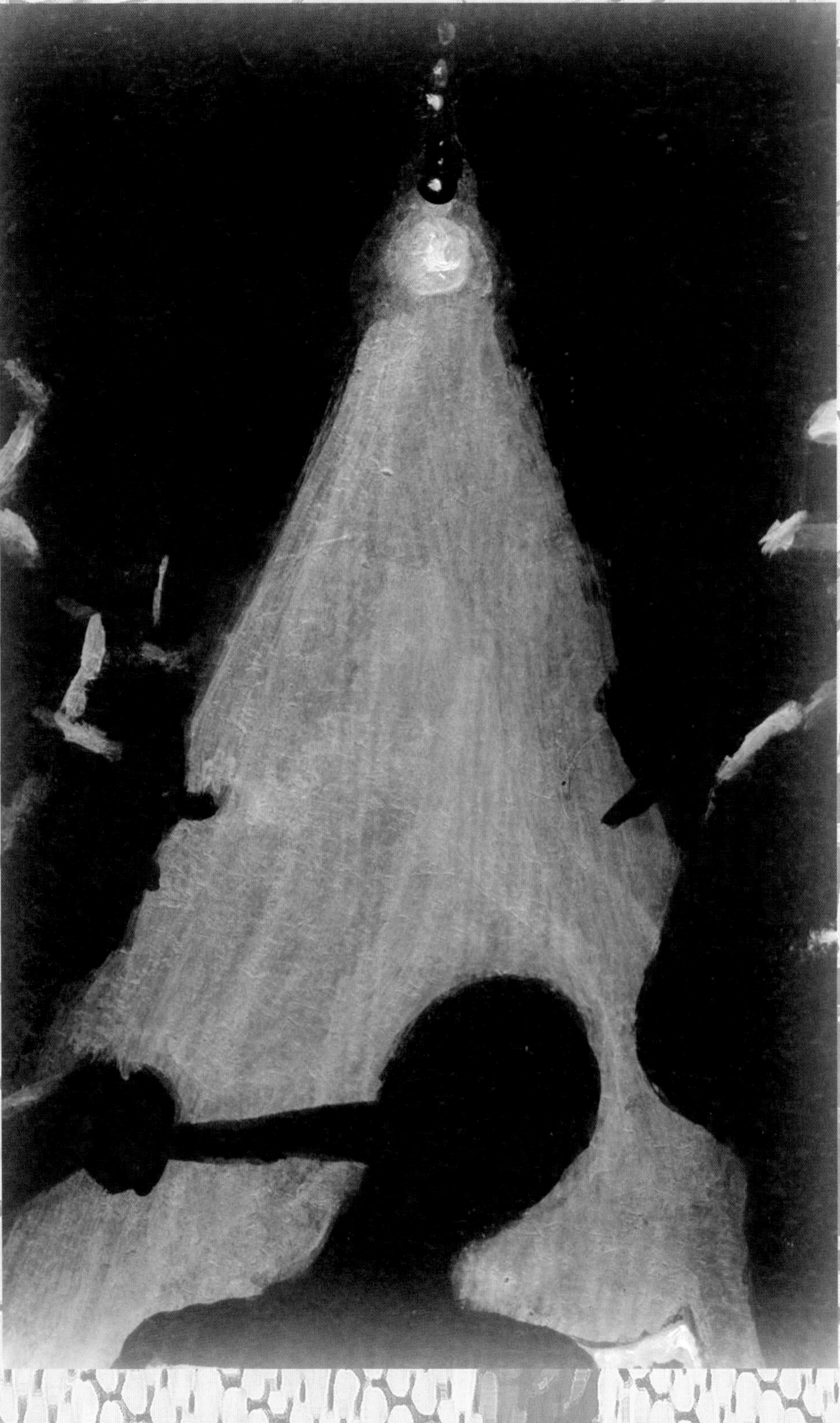

CHAPTER 2

POLITICAL PRISONERS WHO SHAPED WORLD HISTORY

We do not usually think of prisoners as moral leaders. However, political prisoners are often people of extraordinary moral strength; they choose to speak out for their beliefs rather than enjoy the comforts of freedom. For this reason, some of the outstanding political and social leaders of the twentieth and twenty-first centuries were political prisoners for a time. These are their stories.

MAHATMA GANDHI

Mohandas Gandhi was born on October 2, 1869, the youngest of a family with six children, in a small town near Bombay, India. The world knows him today as "Mahatma" Gandhi: Mahatma is an honorary title in the Hindu religion that means "holy" or "wise" and should not be confused with his first name.

As a young man, he was timid and struggled with his grades, but he managed to be the first child in his family to finish high school. After graduation, a friend told Gandhi he should go to England and earn a law degree there. His brother sold land and Gandhi's wife sold her jewelry to pay for his trip to England.

After attaining his degree in law in England, Gandhi went to South Africa to work on his first law case. In that country, something happened that changed the entire direction of Gandhi's life. South Africa at the time practiced apartheid, a practice of race discrimination similar to that of the southern United States at the same time. Gandhi purchased a first-class ticket for the train trip from Durban to Johannesburg. When a train worker came to look at his ticket, he ordered Gandhi to leave first class and move to a poorer car, because the government did not allow "coloreds" (which included people of Indian descent) to travel first class. Gandhi refused to move: he had paid for first class and he insisted on staying there. The train personnel kicked him off the train in the middle of a cold winter night.

Until this incident, Gandhi had shown little interest in politics, but feeling the sting of discrimination, he committed himself to the fight for racial and gender equality. He spent the next twenty-two years opposing discrimination in South Africa. He worked for a newspaper and wrote countless articles that showed how Indians and other people of color were mistreated.

By 1915, Gandhi was forty-five years old and well known for his writing on behalf of justice in South Africa. His native country, India, was a British colony, and many Indians felt Britain was using India selfishly, not for the benefit of Indians. Influential Indians persuaded Gandhi to return to his homeland and work for the freedom of his people.

POLITICAL PRISONERS

Mahatma Gandhi's influence on the entire world continues to be felt.

WHEN A JAIL IS A TEMPLE

From May 1930 to May 1933, the British government imprisoned Gandhi and several of his religious coworkers at Yeravda Prison. Louis Fischer, in his biography *Gandhi: His Life and Message for the World*, writes,

The Mahatma always obeyed the prison rules strictly as well as his own rule not to agitate from prison. Since he could not be a politician, he concentrated on being the saint. . . . After a while, Gandhi began to write down his thoughts on God and the ideal conduct of man: these were later published in a book called *Yeravda Mandir*. Mandir means temple. A jail where God is discussed and worshiped becomes a temple.

Before leaving South Africa, Gandhi had become convinced that ruling governments do not give up power or treat poor people fairly unless people confront them directly. At the same time, he was committed to peace: Gandhi did not believe that mistreated people could achieve anything good through violence. He developed a practice called *Satyagraha*, which means "insistence on truth using nonviolent methods." Satyagraha might involve such methods as strikes, **boycotts**, or peaceful demonstrations. After returning to India, Gandhi began to call on his fellow Indians to use such means to convince Britain to free India. At the same time, he opposed practices common to his fellow Hindus. Most Hindus believed in the caste system, a form of religious-based discrimination against poor people, and many Hindus practiced discrimination against women as well. Gandhi was committed to a society where there would be no discrimination due to race, caste, religion, or gender—all persons would receive equal treatment.

Gandhi's campaign for liberty and equal rights landed him repeatedly in prison. Shall Gandhi Sinha, an expert on Gandhi, writes:

> Gandhi himself was jailed many times, adding up to a total of 7 years during his lifetime, but he did not mind it. He used that period for rest and reflection. He kept writing for his papers. . . . Sometimes he was prevented from writing for his papers, but the government discovered that this created tremendous agitation in the public. The government found Gandhi to be a greater threat while he was imprisoned.

While in Yeravda Prison, Gandhi undertook one of his most important and dramatic political actions. On September 20, 1932, he determined to fast until he died or the British chose to end the practice of separate elections for untouchables (members of India's lowest caste). He believed that separate elections for different castes continued the practice of class discrimination. After six days, as Gandhi was nearing death, the British rulers agreed to end separate elections.

In 1947, Britain freed India from their rule, ending 200 years of domination. It was a major victory for Gandhi and his practices of nonviolent social change. A year later, a fellow Hindu assassinated the Mahatma, angered by Gandhi's insistence on equality between castes. Gandhi, a political prisoner for seven years, had won freedom for all his fellow citizens and set an example of nonviolent change that others, including Dr. Martin Luther King Jr., would follow.

DR. MARTIN LUTHER KING JR.

In 1959, a young Baptist minister traveled to India and spoke with people who had been associates of Mahatma Gandhi. The visit convinced King that Gandhi's philosophy of nonviolence was the only approach appropriate for American blacks to use in their fight to gain their *civil rights*.

> *"One may ask: 'How can you advocate breaking some laws and obeying others?' The answer lies in the fact that there are two types of laws: just and unjust. I would be the first to advocate obeying just laws. One has not only a legal but a moral responsibility to obey just laws. Conversely, one has a moral responsibility to disobey unjust laws. I would agree with St. Augustine that 'an unjust law is no law at all.'"*
> —Dr. Martin Luther King Jr. from *Letter from the Birmingham Jail*

The following year, police in Atlanta, Georgia, arrested King with a group of young people protesting segregation at a department store lunch counter. Although the city dropped charges, a court sentenced King to serve time at Reidsville State Prison Farm on the excuse that he had violated his probation for a minor traffic ticket issued several months earlier. People around the country expressed their concern and anger at this jailing, and blamed President Dwight Eisenhower for failing to intervene. John F. Kennedy, the Democratic presidential nominee, used his influence to get Dr. King released.

In Birmingham, Alabama, in the spring of 1963, Dr. King and his followers continued their campaign to end segregation. Their protests gained sympathy around the nation when news reports showed police turning dogs and fire hoses on the unarmed demonstrators. The police jailed Dr. King along with large numbers of his supporters. While imprisoned, Dr. King wrote one his best-known works, *Letter from the Birmingham Jail*, which explained the methods used by the civil rights movement.

Martin Luther King Jr. (seen here with President Lyndon B. Johnson in the background) was willing to face prison and even death for the cause of justice.

The prison on Robben Island where Nelson Mandela spent almost thirty years

NELSON MANDELA

Nelson Mandela, the former president of South Africa and a Nobel Prize winner, says his greatest pleasure is watching the sun set while listening to classical music. Why does he take such pleasure in ordinary moments? For twenty-seven years, Mandela was a political prisoner, locked alone during daytime hours and denied the pleasures of music.

Nelson Rolihlahla Mandela was born in a village near Umtata in the nation of South Africa on July 18, 1918. He went to school, earned his law degree, and as a young man joined the African National Congress (ANC), an organization dedicated to ending the unjust system of apartheid that controlled every aspect of South African life. Apartheid, or "separation," forced the majority of South Africans—native people of color—to live in inferior homes, attend inferior schools, and receive inferior medical care compared to their white minority fellow citizens, who ran the government and army.

*As I walked through those gates I felt—even at the age of seventy-one—
that my life was beginning anew. My ten thousand days of imprisonment
were at last over.*
—Nelson Mandela, describing his day of release from prison

Influenced by Gandhi's success freeing India by nonviolent means, the ANC at first attempted to follow the Indian's peaceful methods in their struggle for equality. However, the white government responded to their attempts with sometimes-brutal force. The government banned, arrested, and briefly imprisoned Mandela for his nonviolent attempts at justice. By the 1960s, government actions forced Mandela to live underground. He wore disguises, hid away from his family, and worked secretively to organize protests. Finally, in 1961, Mandela and other ANC leaders decided that nonviolence was not going to achieve their freedom: "It was only when all else had failed, when all channels of peaceful protest had been barred to us, that the decision was made to embark on violent forms of political struggle . . . the Government had left us no other choice."

Shortly after the ANC began their armed struggle for freedom, the government captured Mandela and sentenced him to life in prison. He started his prison years in the notorious Robben Island Prison, a maximum-security prison on a small island near Cape Town. In April 1984, the government transferred Mandela to Pollsmoor Prison in Cape Town, and then in December 1988, they moved him again to the Victor Verster Prison near Paarl, from which they eventually released him on February 11, 1990.

In his autobiography, Mandela recalls entering his cell on Robben Island:

> When I lay down, I could feel the wall with my feet and my head grazed the concrete at the other side. The width was about six feet. . . . I was forty-six years old, a political prisoner with a life sentence, and that small cramped space was to be my home for I knew not how long.

Although Robben Island was the harshest facility in the South African prison system, Mandela says, "I never thought that a life sentence truly meant life and that I would die behind bars . . . I always knew that someday I would once again feel the grass underneath my feet and walk in the sunshine as a free man." There were moments that tried the great man's soul: receiving news of his son's death in an auto crash and his wife's imprisonment for her role in the freedom struggle.

Finally, after almost three decades, world condemnation forced the South African government to free Mandela. Four years later, Mandela became the first president elected after *all* the citizens of South Africa had voted, black and white, in a new nation freed from the oppression of apartheid.

VACLAV HAVEL

Famous playwright, internationally published author, leader of a movement to free his country from communism, last president of Czechoslovakia, and first president of the Czech Republic: Vaclav Havel has had an amazing life. Yet it has not been without suffering; for over five years, he was a political prisoner.

Suspicious of his family background, the Communist Party denied Havel the opportunities of a college education, so he took a correspondence course in drama instead. As a young man, he wrote a number of successful plays, married his wife Olga, and worked for the anticommunist magazine *Tvar*.

State authorities imprisoned Havel briefly in 1977 and longer in 1979. In prison, he feared for his life under the custody of a man he describes as a "much-feared, half-demented warden." The warden once sighed and told Havel, "Hitler did things differently—he gassed vermin like you right away!" Havel knew imprisonment would be bearable only if he could "breathe some positive significance into it," so he poured himself into his letters to his wife. These letters later became a popular book, *Letters to Olga*, which has been published in a number of languages.

Authorities offered Havel the chance to leave prison if he would also leave the country, but he refused to do so because he was committed to democracy for the Czech people. In late 1983, Havel developed a life-threatening illness. This, coupled with pressure from foreign supporters on the Czech government, led the communists to release him. After serving time as a political prisoner, Havel had earned a deserved reputation for his commitment to freedom, a factor that has led to his later outstanding political career.

POLITICAL PRISONERS

CHAPTER 3

POLITICAL PRISONERS UNDER FASCISM AND COMMUNISM

There may be times when we are powerless to prevent injustice, but there must never be a time when we fail to protest.
—Holocaust survivor and author Elie Wiesel

ELIE WIESEL

Never shall I forget that night, the first night in camp, which has turned my life into one long night. . . . Never shall I forget that smoke. Never shall I forget the little faces of the children, whose bodies I saw turned into wreaths of smoke beneath a silent blue sky. Never shall I forget those flames which consumed my faith forever.

So writes Elie Wiesel, recounting life in a Holocaust death camp, in his book titled *Night*.

In the twentieth century, there were three powerful ***totalitarian*** governments: the National Socialist (Nazi) government that ruled Germany from 1933 to 1945, the communist government of the Soviet Union that ruled Russia and surrounding nations from 1917 to 1991, and the communist government that has ruled China from 1949 until today. Each of these governments depended on imprisonment as a primary means of political control, and each committed crimes against their own citizens on a massive scale.

Elie Wiesel was born in Sighet, Transylvania, on September 30, 1928. He enjoyed childhood in his Jewish neighborhood that was rich in faith, in community activities, and in loving families. All that changed, however, in 1944 when Nazis rounded up this Jewish community and deported them to concentration camps. The Nazis took Wiesel and his father to Auschwitz, separating them from Wiesel's mother and younger sister, Tzipora. Wiesel was fifteen at the time, and he never saw his mother or younger sister again. Although Wiesel is uniquely famous for his talented writing about the horrors of those years, his experience was far, far from unique: more than six million of his fellow Jews died in the Nazi death camps.

After the war, Wiesel vowed never to write about his Holocaust experiences, but in 1955, after meeting the French Catholic novelist and Nobel laureate Francois Mauriac, he decided to write *Night*. Since then, he has dedicated himself to making sure that the world will never forget what the Nazis did to the Jewish people and others, so that such ***heinous*** things will not happen again. He has published more than thirty books, earned the Nobel Peace Prize, been appointed to chair the President's Commission on the Holocaust, and awarded the Congressional Gold Medal of Achievement. Wiesel's experiences cause him to feel concern for political prisoners around the world. He traveled to the USSR in 1965 and described the situation of Jews in that communist state in a book titled *The Jews of Silence*. Since then, he has worked to bring awareness of political prisoners in the Soviet Union, South Africa, Vietnam, Biafra, and Bangladesh.

POLITICAL PRISONERS

> *We must take sides. Neutrality helps the oppressor, never the victim.*
> —Elie Wiesel

ALEXANDER SOLZHENITSYN

Literary critics regard Alexander Solzhenitsyn as one of the great writers of the twentieth century; the rest of the world honors him as an eloquent representative for human rights. His life, with its hardships and punishments, represents the lives of thousands of Russian citizens during the same years. He was born in 1918, six months after his father died fighting for Russia in World War I; his mother, who made her living as a typist, raised him. As a teen, Solzhenitsyn hoped to become a writer, but poverty forced him to go to a local college and study mathematics instead. Later, Solzhenitsyn reflected:

> I would probably not have survived the eight years in camps if I had not, as a mathematician, been transferred to a so-called *sharashia*, where I spent four years. . . . If I had had a literary education it is quite likely that I should not have survived these ordeals.

Solzhenitsyn served in the Soviet Army during World War II, fighting on the front line until his own government arrested him in February 1945. He later described the reason for this arrest: "I was arrested on the grounds of what the censorship had found during the years 1944–45 in my correspondence with a school friend, mainly because of certain disrespectful remarks about Stalin."

Prisoners in the Gulag's work camps often died from the harsh conditions and brutal treatment.

A FAMOUS AUTHOR YET LACKING FREEDOM

During his years of imprisonment and exile, Solzhenitsyn had been writing about his experiences, but he did not dare to share his work with the public for fear of losing his life. However, not releasing his work troubled him, and in 1961, he published *One Day in the Life of Ivan Denisovich*, a detailed account of daily life in the Gulag. Communist authorities immediately banned the book, but copies were smuggled to the free world, and Solzhenitsyn the writer became famous in the West. As a result, Solzhenitsyn was awarded the Nobel Prize for literature in 1970, but he was unable to claim the prize in person due to government restrictions.

He spent the next eight years in what the Soviet government called "Special Camps." The rest of the world called them the Gulag, and despite the government's nice-sounding name, more than a million political prisoners died from brutal treatment in these incarceration centers.

KGB officers arrested Solzhenitsyn again in 1974 and brought him to Lefortovo Prison. They stripped him, questioned him, and charged him with treason. The next day, the Soviet government deprived Solzhenitsyn of his citizenship and deported him to West Germany. From 1975 to 1995, he chose to live in Vermont, in the United States, then, after the Soviet Union ended its totalitarian reign, he returned to his homeland in 1995.

Despite all the ways he suffered under communism, Solzhenitsyn does not believe that any political party is the major cause of evil in the world. He believes that every person is partially good and partially evil,

Alexander Solzhenitsyn

and therefore each person must undertake to conquer the evil in his or her own heart. His sufferings as a political prisoner and his ability to turn those into powerful writing have made Solzhenitsyn one of the greatest writers and thinkers of his time.

HARRY WU

For nineteen years, Harry Wu was a political prisoner in China's *laogai*, a vast system of deprivation and punishment. Wu survived against

Harry Wu

incredible odds, and then found his way to the United States. Once in America, he did something even more incredible: Wu risked his life and freedom by returning to China in order to do undercover work documenting the continuing mistreatment of prisoners there.

Wu was raised in Shanghai and influenced by his strict father and kindly stepmother. As a young man, he learned his father's Buddhist customs and the teachings of Italian priests at St. Francis School. These religious teachings later proved to be important. He said, "The sense that human beings are connected to a God, that we should treat one another as God's children, helped sustain me in the dreadful years to come."

In 1949, the Communist Party took over China. For the next seven years, Wu tried to be a "good" communist, yet he was unable to keep quiet when he saw injustices. In 1960, a party officer walked into the college classroom where Wu was studying and arrested him. He would spend the next nineteen years as a prisoner.

Wu spent almost two decades in the "laogai," a word that means "reform through labor." In his autobiography, Wu says:

> *Laogai*—the phrase burns my soul, makes me crazy, makes me want to grab Americans and Europeans and Australians and Japanese by the shirt and scream, "Don't you know what's going on over there?" I want the word laogai to be known all over the world in the same way that gulag has become synonymous with the horrors of Stalin's prison system.

The laogai are prisons doubling as factories, where prisoners "have been virtually reduced to slaves." According to Wu's Laogai Research Foundation, in 2005, there were four to six million Chinese citizens held in these camps. The foundation also claims that, since the inception of the laogai, 40 to 50 million people have been imprisoned. "Almost everyone in China is related to someone or has known someone who has been forced to serve a lengthy sentence in the confines of the Laogai."

In the prison system, Wu battled for his life. As soon as he entered a camp, the guards showed him the bodies of prisoners hung up on meat hooks—the punishment for those who disobeyed their captors. Wu learned to eat captured rats and snakes in order to ***stave off*** starvation.

POLITICAL PRISONERS

A laogai camp in China; this one holds about a thousand prisoners who are forced to produce cement and stone materials.

When a friend of Wu's was nearing starvation, he persuaded a guard to bring his friend extra rations. Unfortunately, the extra food was too much for Wu's *emaciated* friend to digest, and he died "from the surprise of real food." Enraged, Wu cried out in anger at God. Someone—he says it may have been the voice of God or of his father— replied, "Survive. Get through this. Someday you will tell the world."

Wu was beaten by guards, starved, and humiliated, yet survive he did. In 1979, changes in the communist system caused the government to release many victims of the laogai. Wu says, "I was forty-two years old. For the first time in my life, I was a free man." However, life in the communist state outside of prison camp was only relatively free. Wu knew party informants were always watching, making sure he did not step out of line with the government; he would have to leave his native country to enjoy

Henry Wu returned to China secretly so that he could report to the rest of the world the conditions in the laogai.

a truly free life. In 1983, he witnessed a public execution. He reflected, "I was stunned at how organized it was. This government could not feed its people, but it could kill forty-five people in unison for . . . entertainment and education." This furthered Wu's determination to get out of China.

When Wu received an invitation to speak in Berkeley, California, he jumped at the opportunity to leave China, and at the time, he had no intention of ever returning. Life in the United States was not easy at first. He had to sleep in a park some nights, and he worked making donuts, even though he was a highly educated professional in China.

In 1986, Wu had an opportunity to speak about his experiences as a prisoner of conscience in China. He was shocked to learn that Americans did not know anything about the Chinese prison system, and in some cases, they disbelieved him. Although he had just married and was beginning to experience a comfortable life in the United States, Harry Wu decided he would have to take some big risks in order to provide the West with evidence of the cruel treatment endured by millions of his fellow Chinese.

Between 1991 and 1995, Wu returned to China four times, secretly filming and documenting conditions of political prisoners in the laogai. In 1991, he posed as a prison guard and carried a hidden camera to produce evidence for the CBS news program *60 Minutes*, documenting that Chinese prisoners were used as slave laborers producing products for export to the West. In 1994, he posed as a wealthy American seeking an organ donor for a sick uncle. He visited twenty-seven labor camps, proving that China was killing prisoners in order to provide organs for wealthy recipients.

In 1995, the Chinese Communist Party arrested Wu, who was then an American citizen, for spying in China. For sixty-six days, letters and statements of protest came to China from all around the globe. The U.S. Congress passed resolutions condemning the arrest and urging President Clinton to work for Wu's freedom. Due to worldwide concern, the Chinese government gave Wu a mock trial, then expelled him from the country. Back in the United States, Harry Wu continues to seek democracy and freedom for his homeland.

WEI JINGSHENG

Dear Deng Xiaoping:

I've written to you so many times now that I'm probably beginning to get on your nerves and you're wondering, "Why can't this guy just sit in prison quietly?" This appears to be a real problem, but it is not entirely my fault. I am very capable of staying quiet, but if people don't allow me to be, then I can also be very unquiet. . . . My endless letters and constant badgering are in the tradition of "oppressive government drives the people to rebel."

—A letter from prison from Wei Jingsheng to China's leader,
   November 3, 1989

POLITICAL PRISONERS

Mao Tse-tung was the leader of the Cultural Revolution in China.

Wei Jingsheng was born one year after the beginning of Communist Party rule in China. His parents were proud, longtime members of the party, and they raised him as a member of its "inner circle," thereby allowing him to receive an education in China's most prestigious schools.

In 1966, the "Cultural Revolution" took place, a time when innumerable Chinese citizens were humiliated, imprisoned, or executed over trifling offenses against the Communist Party. The revolution began when Mao Tse-tung—or Chairman Mao as he was called—decided to remove less radical elements of the party. Young *zealous* party members formed units of the "Red Guard" to purge "Old Guard" elements from the country. The Red Guard forced educated and wealthy members of society to leave their jobs and schools in order to live in poverty in the countryside and "learn from the peasants." Eventually, the Cultural Revolution spun out of control. It became a national witch hunt as countless people were accused of disloyalty to the new order. As time went on, the situation spun even more out of control, becoming a civil war, with units of the Red Guard battling each other for control of the country. Wei Jingsheng traveled through the country during this turbulent time, and he witnessed firsthand how the Chinese people suffered under communism; this was the beginning of his loss of faith in the government. He became involved with a magazine protesting the lack of freedom in China.

In 1979, the communist leadership charged Wei Jingsheng with "counter-revolution propaganda and agitation." He spoke in his own defense at the trial, and friends copied down his words, which foreign presses translated and released outside of China. The government kept Wei on death row for eight months, then in solitary confinement for the next five years. The Chinese government incarcerated him in two more forced labor camps where guards treated him very harshly. He suffered from several serious illnesses, which authorities did not treat properly. In 1993, the government released Wei Jingsheng, but six months later, they arrested and tried him again. Authorities convicted Wei of "counter-revolution" and sentenced him to serve another fourteen years in the laogai system.

After a total of eighteen years in prison, in 1997, the Chinese government took Wei Jingsheng from his prison and put him on a plane to the

Wei Jingsheng continues to work for human rights in China.

United States, the result of a deal between President Clinton and Chinese president Jiang ZeMin. Since 1993, Wei Jingsheng has been nominated seven times for the Nobel Peace Prize. As of 2005, Wei Jingsheng continues to work tirelessly to promote democratization and the improvement of human rights in China.

It would be nice to think that with the turning of the century and the beginning of a new millennium would come an enlightenment making the imprisoning of those with contrary beliefs obsolete. Unfortunately, that has not happened, and people continue to go to prison and face other harsh punishments for their principles.

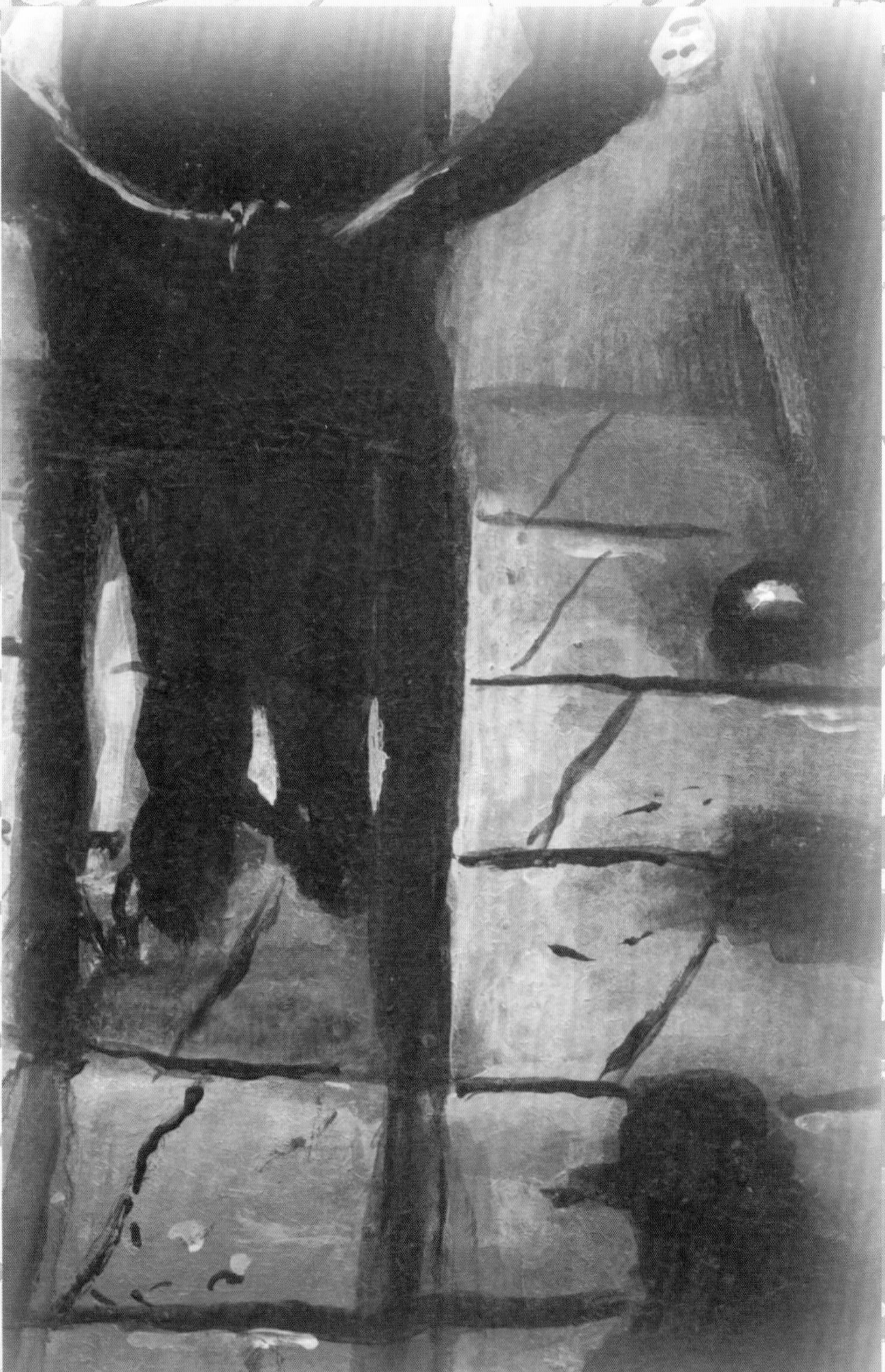

CHAPTER 4

PROMINENT POLITICAL PRISONERS OF THE TWENTY-FIRST CENTURY

AUNG SAN SUU KYI: BURMA'S HEROIC PRISONER FOR FREEDOM

My home . . .

where I was born and raised

used to be warm and lovely

now filled with darkness and horror.

My family . . .

whom I had grown with

used to be cheerful and lively

Aung San Suu Kyi

A COUNTRY WITH DISPUTED NAMES

The name of the country was once Burma, but in 1989, the army, which ruled the country, officially changed its name to Myanmar. Opponents of the military government, both within and outside the country, argue that the government does not have the authority to change the country's name. The United Nations recognizes the name Myanmar, but several countries—including the United States, the United Kingdom, and Canada—still refer to Myanmar as Burma.

> *now living with fear and terror.*
> *My friends . . .*
> *whom I shared my life with*
> *used to be pure and merry*
> *now living with wounded heart.*
> *A free bird . . .*
> *which is just freed*
> *used to be caged*
> *now flying with an olive branch*
> *for the place it loves.*
> *A free bird towards a Free Burma.*
> —Aung San Suu Kyi (from her Web site)

On her sixtieth birthday, June 19, 2005, Aung San Suu Kyi (pronounced like Awn Sawn Sue Chee) received well wishes and greetings from politicians and celebrities around the world. "I send my best wishes to Aung San Suu Kyi for her 60th birthday," said U.S. president George W. Bush,

and his sentiments were echoed by UN Secretary General Kofi Annan, fellow Nobel prize winner South African Bishop Desmond Tutu, exiled Buddhist leader the Dalai Lama, and Czech president and former political prisoner Vaclav Havel. Rock stars joined political and religious leaders in their birthday wishes. In a Dublin concert, rock band REM broadcast a live sixtieth-birthday tribute to her. REM lead singer Michael Stipe said, "We want to wish you a happy 60th birthday filled with hope and say that we deeply respect your profound commitment to the people of Burma. . . . And we pray with our hearts that by your 61st birthday, you will walk free among your people." Likewise, Irish rock band U2 sang "Happy Birthday" to the Burmese hero during a sold-out concert, before launching into their song "Walk On," which they had composed years before in her honor.

What did Aung San Suu Kyi think of all these well wishes, or did she even know of them? No one can say, for she spent her birthday, as she spent many days before, under strict house arrest. She cannot leave her dwelling, the government has disconnected her telephone, and her only human contact is with a doctor she sees monthly. Although she is famous internationally, has won the Nobel Peace Prize, and was voted by more than 80 percent of her fellow Burmese citizens to serve as their leader, Suu Kyi is (as of December 2005) a political prisoner. To understand her story, we must learn something about the country of Burma (also called Myanmar), and her father, Aung San.

Aung San Suu Kyi says, "Burma is one of those countries which seem to have been favored by nature." Writers and travelers have called Burma "the golden land" and "an eastern paradise." It is covered with lush jungle, bordered by blue sea, and favored with a wealth of minerals, precious gems, and stunning architecture. Until the mid-nineteenth century, Burma was a colony of England, although most Burmese desired to rule their own nation. When World War II began, Japanese troops claimed to "liberate" Burma by chasing out the English, but in fact, the Japanese took over the country and ruled it themselves. Burmese freedom fighters joined forces with their former British rulers and fought against the Japanese. When they drove out the Japanese, Burmese leaders and troops insisted on the right to govern their own nation.

The golden land of Myanmar (once called Burma)

Burma was an ancient and proud country that insisted on its right to freedom after World War II.

The most important person in the struggle for Burma's freedom from foreign governments was a general named Aung San. He had organized Burmese fighters to resist the Japanese, and then worked with the British after the war to ensure Burma's freedom. To this day, the Burmese regard Aung San as "the father of his country." Although he is a legendary figure, Aung San did not live to enjoy the freedom he fought for; in 1947, a political rival assassinated him, just months before Britain granted Burma independence.

When he died, Aung San left behind a two-year-old daughter, Aung San Suu Kyi. Parents in Burma rarely name their children after themselves; however, General Aung San broke with tradition, giving his name to his only daughter. Aung San means victory: to add softness to his daughter's name, he drew from his mother's name, Suu, and from his wife's name, Kyi. Put together, the name, Aung San Suu Kyi means "a bright collection of strange victories." It is an unusual name, and its meaning helped give a sense of unusual destiny to the amazing woman who bears it.

Aung San Suu Kyi lived a privileged childhood and young adulthood. After the assassination of General Aung San, the Burmese government appointed Daw Khin Kyi, the general's widow and Suu Kyi's mother, to serve as Burma's ambassador to India. Suu Kyi then went to live in Delhi with her mother. In India, she became aware of Mohandas Gandhi's life and philosophy, knowledge that would influence Aung San Suu Kyi's later efforts for freedom through nonviolent means.

In the 1960s, while a repressive military government took control of Burma, Suu Kyi was studying philosophy, politics, and economics at Oxford College in England. At Oxford, fellow students noted Suu Kyi for both her beauty and her strong morals: she wore traditional Burmese clothes such as the sarong, and once told fellow students that she would never sleep with anyone except her husband, preferring to, "just go to bed hugging my pillow."

While a student in England, she met a fellow scholar named Michael Aris, who was studying Eastern culture and Buddhism; he fell in love with her, but she resisted. Though Suu Kyi graduated and moved to New York to work for the United Nations and Aris took a job working for the royal family of Bhutan, they kept up correspondence. She was falling in love with the handsome British man, but Suu Kyi repeatedly wrote him saying that if they were to marry, her commitment to her own Burmese people might have to come before their marriage. "I only ask one thing," she wrote in one letter, "that should my people need me, you would help me to do my duty by them." He agreed, and in 1972, they both returned to England and married. Soon after, they had two children.

For more than a decade, Aung San Suu Kyi and Michael Aris, along with their children, lived happily together. Then, Suu Kyi received a phone call; her mother was desperately ill in Rangoon, Burma, and would she come to be by her mother's side? She put down the receiver and began to pack. "I had a premonition," Michael later said, "that our lives would change forever."

The Shwedagon Pagoda is one of Myanmar's national landmarks.

Back in Burma, Suu Kyi found her homeland in the middle of a revolution. Thousands of students had begun a movement for democracy, which soon gained broad support. As she was already famous as the daughter of "the father of the country," leaders of the revolutionary movement asked Suu Kyi to speak out in favor of democracy. On July 23, the dictatorial ruler of the country, General Ne Win, announced that he was resigning; Suu Kyi and her fellow citizens were elated, assuming that the people of Burma actually had a chance to take control of their destiny.

On August 8, 1988—known as the "Four Eights," or 8/8/88—student leaders called for a nationwide strike for democracy, and crowds of students, government workers, and monks poured into the streets. In response to this protest, President Sein Lwin ordered troops to fire on the demonstrators. Inflamed by this outrage, Suu Kyi wrote an open letter to the government, proposing democratic elections, and then she prepared for a major public speech.

On August 26, a sea of people filled an open field beneath the Shwedagon Pagoda, the spiritual and architectural heart of Burma, near the burial site of Suu Kyi's exalted father, Aung San. There, people climbed trees to catch a glimpse of Aung San's daughter. Her companions warned Suu Kyi that someone might try to shoot her during the speech, yet she refused to wear a bulletproof vest.

Her speech was electrifying. Despite ***atrocities*** committed by government soldiers, Suu Kyi told the crowd that they must not hate the army, even as they protested military rule. She said that this moment was "the second struggle for national independence," and the crowd of 100,000 men, women, and children shouted their approval.

The following years were a time of great danger, yet great hope in Burma. The government continued its brutal treatment of democratic leaders and activists, yet the majority of people in Burma continued to hope for real elections and democratic change. For almost a year, Suu Kyi traveled throughout the country, speaking relentlessly against the military government and in favor of reform. In April 1989, Suu Kyi and a group of democratic activists were headed for the town of Danubyu

The city of Rangoon, where Suu Kyi was imprisoned

when a group of soldiers blocked their way, pointing automatic rifles at them. "Keep moving," Suu Kyi told her group, and then she spoke calmly to the soldiers: "Let us pass." There were a few tense moments before an officer rushed up and ordered the soldiers to ***stand down.*** Later that evening, Suu Kyi told her fellow activists that if the government killed her, they should use that opportunity "to win democracy and freedom for the country."

On July 20, 1989, soldiers surrounded the office of the democratic party and arrested Suu Kyi. Her eleven-year-old son, Kim, was with her at the time; he asked if the soldiers were going to take her away, and she replied yes. That was the beginning of her first six years of house arrest. Her husband, Michael, was in Scotland for his father's funeral. He hurried to Rangoon, but during the entire six years, the government only allowed him to visit with Suu Kyi twice. He had to live back in Oxford, taking care of the boys and missing his wife whom, he said, was "the warm heart of the Aris household."

Suu Kyi was awarded the Nobel Peace Prize in 1991, but she was unable to accept the prize in person, since she was still under arrest.

For Suu Kyi, missing her husband and children became part of the pain of her daily life. The government wanted to tell people that the democracy leader was depressed and dispirited, therefore she was determined to dress well, stay fit, and act positive. She awoke early each morning, meditated for an hour, exercised on a Nordic Track, kept the house

Suu Kyi was inspired by the principles of Buddha.

clean, listened to the radio, read books, and sewed. She dressed neatly each day, putting flowers in her hair.

In 1990, Suu Kyi's democratic party won 82 percent of the Burmese national election seats. As party chairperson, Aung San Suu Kyi should have been, according to the vote, leader of the Burmese nation. However, the army had no actual intention of honoring the election results; they declared the vote invalid and kept Suu Kyi under house arrest. The following year, she was awarded the Nobel Peace Prize. Because she was still under arrest, her sons accepted the award on her behalf.

In 1995, the military leaders of Burma (by then renamed Myanmar) allowed Suu Kyi what they declared to be "freedom," though she was under continual surveillance and not allowed to leave Rangoon. She continued to speak out against the government and in favor of an open democracy. In 1999, her husband phoned from England with the news that he had been diagnosed with cancer. The Myanmar government would not allow Michael to enter their country, and if Suu Kyi left her country, the government would never allow her to return. Aung San Suu Kyi faced her most difficult choice: to leave and be with her husband for his hour of greatest need, or to stay and continue the fight for a free Burma. Drawing from a life of Buddhist belief and practice, she made her decision by means of prayer and contemplation: "My country first."

An American protest march on behalf of Aung San Suu Kyi

In a *Washington Post* article, Ellen Nakashima relates a sad episode at the end of Michael's life:

> Toward the end of his life, when he was in the hospital, she would try to speak with him every evening. Because her phone line was cut, she arranged to await his call at the home of a diplomat. Military intelligence soon figured it out. One evening, Michael and Suu had just said hello when the line went dead. In a rare moment of utter despair, she burst into tears.

Michael Aris died in 1999. The next year, the government again arrested Suu Kyi and held her for nineteen months.

After her release, Suu Kyi toured the country with other activists. On May 30, 2003, a day since recalled by Burmese freedom activists as "Black Friday," a mob armed with bamboo spears surrounded their vehicles and began smashing open windows. They grabbed activists, stripped them, and beat them. Her fellow activists begged Suu Kyi to flee, but she would not. Her driver gunned their car and raced away from the mob. Burmese activists are convinced this mob attack was a government assassination attempt. Though the Myanmar leadership deny that allegation, it is curious that soldiers stopped her vehicle as soon as it escaped from the mob, and once again Suu Kyi was placed under house arrest.

She remains under arrest as of December 2005. It is a grave embarrassment for the military dictatorship of Myanmar that the daughter of General Aung San, the honorable father of the country, opposes their authority. Consequently, the government forbids anyone to display an image of Aung San Suu Kyi or to speak her name. Since her name has been ***expunged***, the Myanmar government refers to her as "puppet doll," "Mrs. Race destructionist," "that person," or tellingly, "the very specific problem." The Burmese people, fearing punishment from the military yet desiring to honor Suu Kyi, refer to her as "The Lady." Her full name, Aung San Suu Kyi, remains hidden in the hearts of her fellow Burmese citizens, while political and cultural leaders around the world celebrate her dedication to freedom.

POLITICAL PRISONERS

Kurds are a large and distinct ethnic minority in the Middle East, numbering some 25 to 30 million people. They inhabit Iran, Iraq, Syria, and Turkey. In Turkey, Kurds make up 20 percent of the national population, but the founder of modern Turkey, Mustafa Kemal, denied the existence of distinct cultural subgroups in Turkey, and so the Turkish government treats any expression of Turkish ethnicity harshly. For example, until 1991, the use of the Kurdish language was illegal, and to this day, any talk of Kurdish nationalism can result in imprisonment.

LEYLA ZANA: IMPRISONED FOR SPEAKING HER OWN LANGUAGE

Turkish officials released Leyla Zana from prison on June 9, 2004, after a decade of incarceration for the crimes of wearing Kurdish colors on her headband in parliament, and speaking her native Kurdish language.

Leyla Zana was born in a small Kurdish village in Turkey in 1961. While still a teenager, she was married to a much older man who was an activist for Kurdish freedom; he introduced his young wife to the struggle for Kurdish liberation. When she was fifteen, Leyla gave birth to a son, and shortly after, she became the first woman in her town awarded a high school diploma. Five years later, shortly before Leyla gave birth to a daughter, the Turkish government arrested her husband and sentenced

Dissidents like Leyla Zana insist that Kurdish culture should be recognized as a legitimate part of the Turkish nation.

him to thirty years in jail. Undaunted, Leyla continued her education and her work for Kurdish freedom and women's rights in Turkey.

In 1991, Zana became famous in Turkey when she became the first woman from the minority Kurdish ethnic group elected to the Turkish parliament. During her oath of allegiance to Turkey's parliament, Leyla Zana said:

> I swear by my honor and my dignity before the great Turkish people to protect the integrity and independence of the State, the indivisible unity of people and homeland, and the unquestionable and unconditional sovereignty of the people. I swear loyalty to the Constitution. *I take this oath for the brotherhood between the Turkish people and the Kurdish people.*

She spoke the italicized sentence in her native Kurdish tongue. After her election, Leyla Zana dared to speak Kurdish in the Turkish parliament and wear the Kurdish colors in the ribbons in her headband, actions that caused uproar throughout the country and led to her imprisonment. Zana and others have formed a new party, called the Democratic Society Movement, dedicated to defending Kurdish culture as a legitimate part of the Turkish nation.

FATHER THADEUS NGUYEN VAN LY: IMPRISONED FOR PRACTICING HIS RELIGION

Although the title of this book is *Political Prisoners*, it is important to remember that governments imprison people for reasons other than politics. Historically and at present, various governments around the world have persecuted and imprisoned people for practicing their religion. Today, human rights groups accuse nations including Sudan, China, Vietnam, Afghanistan, and Pakistan of violating their citizens' rights to religious freedom.

The lush land of Vietnam has seen much violence.

Father Thadeus Nguyen Van Ly is a Vietnamese Catholic priest who has suffered because the government opposed his religious beliefs. According to the advocacy group Freedom Now, which worked to secure Father Nguyen Van Ly's release, "Since 1977, the Government of Vietnam has repeatedly arrested, harassed, and jailed Father Ly for his advocacy of religious freedom." Several advocacy groups protested Father Ly's mistreatment, resulting in a November 2004 resolution by the U.S. Congress that asked the Vietnamese government to release the priest. Three months later, Vietnamese authorities released Father Ly.

On June 20, 2005, Vietnamese prime minister Phan Van Kai made a historic visit to the United States. On that same day, Father Thadeus Nguyen Van Ly submitted written testimony to the International Relations Committee of the House of Representatives in Washington, D.C., documenting his own mistreatment and the mistreatment of other re-

Father Thadeus Nguyen Van Ly

ligionists at the hands of the Vietnamese government. Commenting on the written testimony, Representative Chris Smith said the United States will keep watching Vietnam to see if religious freedom is honored by that nation in the future.

THE PANCHEN LAMA GEDHUN: A CHILD IMPRISONED BECAUSE OF HIS ROLE IN THE BUDDHIST FAITH

The imprisonment of the Panchen Lama is so bizarre and tragic it is almost unbelievable. The story involves a conquered nation, a reincarnated religious leader, and a communist government attempt to control the spiritual beliefs of the Tibetan people. In 1950, the People's Republic of China announced its intention to "liberate" Tibet, and 40,000 Chinese troops invaded and took control of the little nation. A national uprising nine years later led to the slaughter of 400,000 Tibetans. This led the Chinese to impose their language and education system on the country, and to destroy thousands of Buddhist monasteries.

On May 14, 1995, the Dalai Lama (the spiritual leader of Tibet in exile) declared that a six-year-old Tibetan boy, Gedhun Choekyi Nyima, was the reincarnation of religious leader Panchen Rinpoche, who had died six years previously. Panchen means "Great Scholar," and Lama is a word Tibetans use for a religious teacher. Tibetan Buddhists believe that the Panchen Lama is the protector of all the world's living beings. Three days later, Chinese authorities kidnapped Gedhun and his family, "for his safety." In the decade since, no one has seen or heard anything of Gedhun or his family. Six months after they kidnapped this young boy and his family, the Chinese government forced monks of the Tibetan Buddhist community to meet in Beijing. There, the Chinese presented another young boy they called "the real Panchen Lama." One monk chose suicide rather than accept a religious leader imposed by communist authorities.

As of mid-2005, the Chinese government's appointed Panchen Lama is giving speeches in Tibet, praising the Chinese government for helping the Tibetan people, and claiming that Tibetans enjoy full political and religious freedom—statements vigorously denied by Tibetans living in

POLITICAL PRISONERS

The Dalai Lama is the exiled spiritual leader of Tibet.

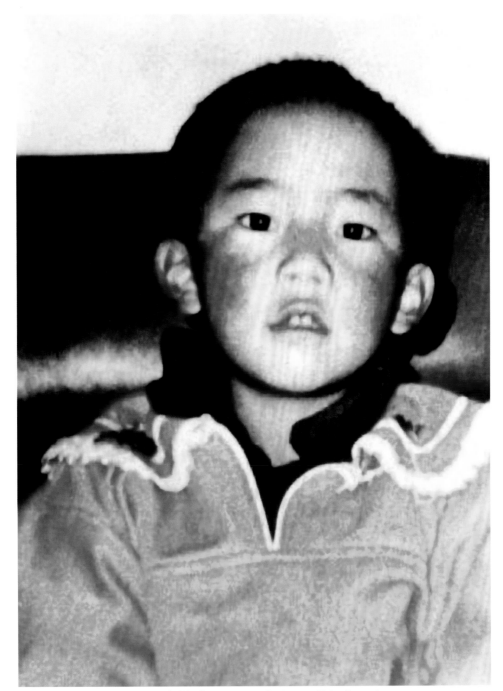

Panchen Lama Gedhun, a child who was caught in a political maelstrom

exile. Meanwhile, the Chinese government claims that Gedhun and his family are "free, happy and healthy," living by their own choice at an undisclosed location in China. The government has given no evidence and no specific information to support this claim. In private Tibetan homes and monasteries today there are innumerable portraits of the six-year-old Panchen Lama—not the boy chosen by the Chinese government, but rather the missing child chosen by the Dalai Lama. Buddhists, exiled Tibetans, and numerous supporters around the world continue to request proven information about Gedhun, his location, and his condition.

Not every political prisoner is held in a foreign country. Although the use of the term "political prisoner" may be controversial when used in connection with the United States, there are those incarcerated in the United States who claim the only reason for their imprisonment is their beliefs.

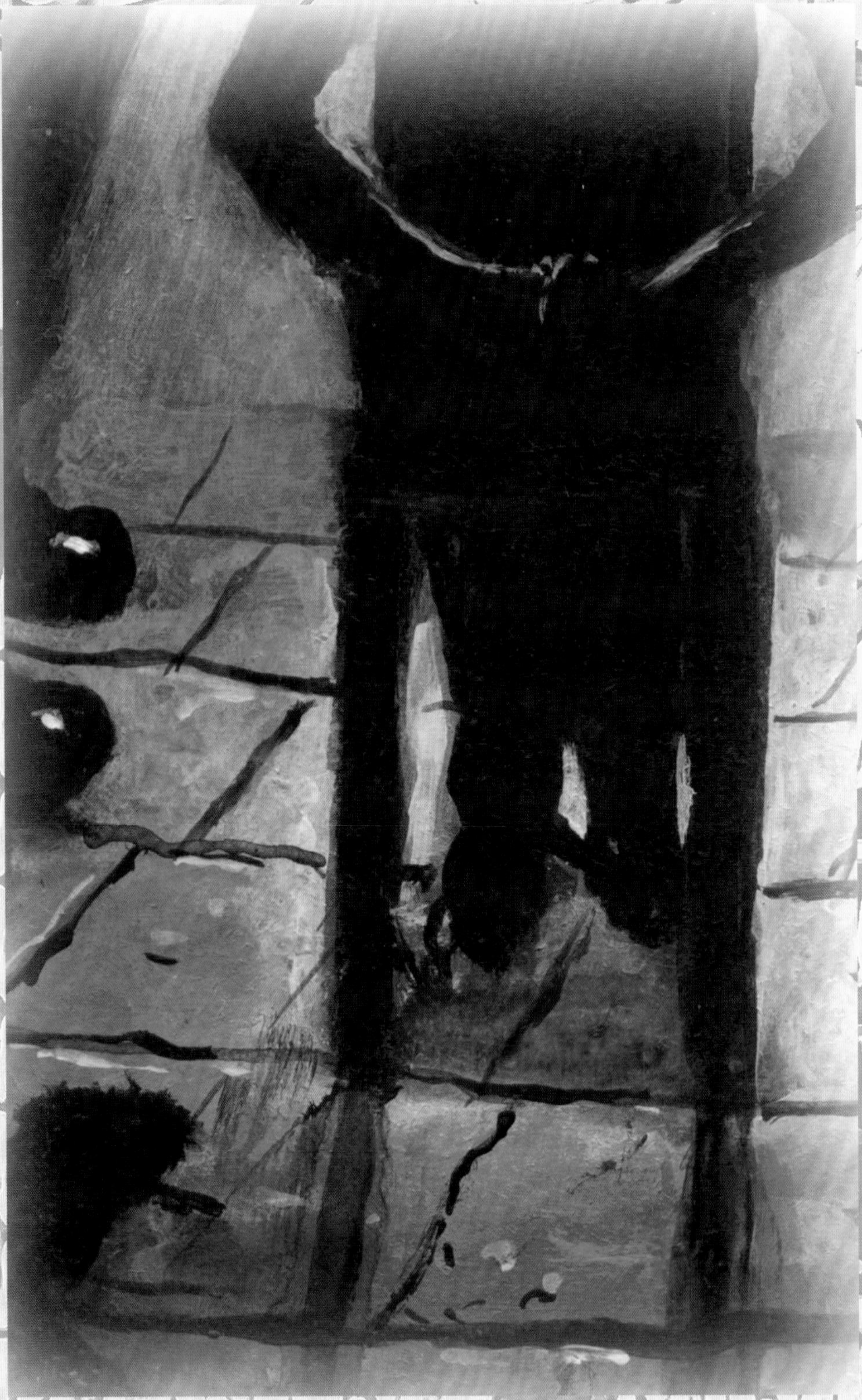

CHAPTER 5

POLITICAL PRISONERS IN THE UNITED STATES?

As the question mark in the chapter title indicates, there is debate whether the term "political prisoners" should apply to certain cases involving the United States. There are differing perspectives on each of these controversial issues.

POLITICAL PRISONERS

Mumia Abu-Jamal

MUMIA ABU-JAMAL

U.S. Supreme Court Justice Harry Blackmun wrote in 1994, "Even under the most sophisticated death penalty statutes, race continues to play a major role in determining who shall live and who shall die."

Legal defender Leonard Weinglass says, "The fight to save Mumia from legal lynching has become the focal point of struggle against the racist death penalty in the U.S." However, the Fraternal Order of Police states, "Danny Faulkner was a good and decent man and an honorable police officer. He was brutally murdered and his killer is Mumia Abu-Jamal." The Abu-Jamal case has attracted the attention of celebrities including Spike Lee, Paul Newman, and Maya Angelou, as well as organizations from as far away as France and Denmark. Defenders say Abu-Jamal is a political prisoner, framed by the Philadelphia police; others say he is a common murderer.

There are a few facts on which everyone agrees. At 4 A.M. on December 9, 1981, in downtown Philadelphia, police officer Daniel Faulkner stopped a car and arrested its driver, William Cook, for driving in the wrong direction. A short time later, other officers came on the scene and found Officer Faulkner lying dead in the street with bullets in his back and face. Nearby, slumped in a pool of his own blood, Cook's brother, Mumia Abu-Jamal, lay wounded by a bullet from Officer Faulkner's gun.

Abu-Jamal was already famous in Philadelphia as a radical black activist. At the age of fifteen, he began writing articles for the Black Panthers. By 1981, he had become a radical journalist who sought to expose corruption and mistreatment of minorities in the city. Abu-Jamal was under surveillance by the FBI and the Philadelphia police for his activism.

His distrust of police stemmed in part from an incident when he protested racist presidential candidate George Wallace; a group of whites were beating Jamal when some police officers arrived on the scene. Abu-Jamal believed the police officers would rescue him, but instead they joined in beating him.

Abu-Jamal sought to defend himself at his trial for Faulkner's murder, and the judge at first agreed. After what the judge called some unruly

Jurors were frightened by Abu-Jamal's dreadlocks.

behavior (and the contention that Abu-Jamal's dreadlocks frightened some jurors), the judge ordered him to be defended by an attorney. Regardless, the jury found him guilty and sentenced him to death. For twenty-four years, he has sought to escape the death penalty and protested his innocence. His supporters claim there are at least eight reasons Abu-Jamal should receive a new trial: questions include the validity of the witnesses, the selection of the jury, the actions of the jury, the

Are the scales of justice unequal for people of color?

POLITICAL PRISONERS IN THE UNITED STATES?

Blacks are more apt to be arrested than whites.

actions of the judge, and the ***dubious*** nature of some evidence. Those who support the guilty verdict respond to each claim with assertions that the Philadelphia legal system conducted the trial properly. For more than two decades, the case against Mumia Abu-Jamal has divided Philadelphia and the nation, and raised questions regarding the fairness of American justice.

Abu-Jamal's case is emotional in part because it represents a larger issue: the gap between treatment of whites and blacks in the U.S. justice system. In 2003, 44 percent of state and federal prisoners were

Do American Indians receive the same brand of justice as whites?

Leonard Peltier

black, compared with 35 percent white, 19 percent Latino, and 2 percent other races. Furthermore, blacks are more likely to receive the death penalty. Black men alone make up over 42 percent of all death row prisoners, though they account for only 6 percent of people living in the United States. Although it is a minority view, some critics of the U.S. justice system contend that all blacks incarcerated are political prisoners, since issues of racism and inequality, not connected with individual cases, are a factor in their sentencing.

LEONARD PELTIER

"My name is Leonard Peltier.
I am a Lakota and Anishnabe
And I am living in the United States penitentiary,
Which is the swiftest growing
Indian reservation in the country . . . ."
—from the Free Leonard Peltier Committee Web site

Like that of Abu-Jamal, the case of Leonard Peltier divides observers into two camps. Some see Peltier as a killer, rightfully convicted of killing two law enforcement agents. On the other hand, a large number of supporters around the world, including former attorney general of the United States Ramsey Clark, Nobel Peace Prize winner Bishop Desmond Tutu of South Africa, filmmaker Robert Redford, and numerous Native activists proclaim Peltier's innocence. Peltier says his only guilt is that he was born an American Indian.

In 1975, the Pine Ridge Indian Reservation in South Dakota was experiencing a wave of violence. Activists with the American Indian Movement (AIM) were in conflict with supporters of the tribal council. The tribal council and allegedly the FBI and Bureau of Indian Affairs had armed a group of supporters known as the Guardians of the Oglala Nation (GOONS). Over two years, there were more than sixty murders on the reservation. Many of these deaths remain unsolved. The mid-'70s

were a time of terrible pain for the people at Pine Ridge, and many mysteries remain concerning the events of that time. Leonard Peltier's incarceration is one legacy of what some still call "the reign of terror."

All accounts agree that agents Jack Coler and Ronald Williams drove onto the Jumping Bull Compound of the reservation at a time when Leonard Peltier and several companions from AIM were camping there to protect a family. There was a firefight. Peltier claims he and his friends were uncertain who the combatants were, and they later found the two agents dead after the battle. The FBI claims Peltier himself killed the agents. Large numbers of FBI agents and GOONS then moved into the compound. Following an eagle, Peltier and his companions escaped, eventually arriving in Canada. Later, Canada sent Peltier back to the United States to face trial. Separate courts tried two of Peltier's AIM friends who were with him that day and they were found not guilty by reason of self-defense.

Peltier, however, was tried, convicted of murder, and sentenced to two life sentences. Peltier's supporters claim the trial was unfair. They contend that the government's key witness, allegedly Peltier's girlfriend, was someone Peltier had never even met before the trial, and that the alleged murder weapon was never in Peltier's possession. Government supporters in turn dispute all these claims, and allege the trial was fair and just. Like Abu-Jamal, many consider Peltier a political prisoner since his case involves larger issues of justice.

GUANTANAMO BAY

Guantanamo is a U.S. military base on Cuban soil, which has been operational for over a century. A 1903 agreement with Cuba gives the United States "complete jurisdiction and control" of the Guantanamo Bay. In recent years, the site has become the subject of international controversy for its use as a prison, holding detainees from Afghanistan and other countries. As of July 2005, there are 520 prisoners, mostly alleged terrorists, in the facility.

The U.S. military base at Guantanamo Bay

Gitmo is on Cuban soil rather than American.

"Gitmo," as it is commonly called, has become a flashpoint for international controversy regarding the treatment and rights of prisoners. The U.S. government's stated position is that the United States is in a war and, therefore, must treat terrorist enemies in ways that differ from ordinary imprisonment; this will protect the United States from attack and help get information vital to national security. On the other hand, international groups such as the Red Cross and Amnesty International, as well as some U.S. citizens including former president Jimmy Carter, believe that violations of international standards at Guantanamo harm American interests and are unworthy of its ideals.

TORTURE AT GITMO?

There have been multiple allegations of mistreatment of prisoners at Guantanamo Bay. Three British citizens, released in 2004 without any charges ever filed against them, allege they suffered torture, sexual humiliation, and denial of religious freedom at the facility. Moazzam Begg, freed in January 2005, after nearly three years in captivity at Guantanamo, accuses American soldiers of torturing detainees from Afghanistan and Pakistan, claiming he "witnessed two people get beaten so badly that I believe it caused their deaths." These allegations have not been confirmed, as of July 2005. On November 30, 2004, the *New York Times* released excerpts from a report by the International Committee of the Red Cross, stating that conditions at Guantanamo were "tantamount to torture." A 2005 report by Amnesty International likened Guantanamo Bay to the Gulag of Soviet Russia, alleging widespread abuse of prisoners. A June 2005 *New York Times* article quoted an FBI agent as saying, "On a couple of occasions, I entered interview rooms to find a detainee chained hand and foot in a fetal position to the floor, with no chair, food or water. Most times they had urinated or defecated on themselves and had been left there for 18, 24 hours or more."

The U.S. government disputes all these claims. In June 2005, Vice President Dick Cheney defended conditions at Guantanamo, saying, "They're very well treated down there. They're living in the tropics. They're well fed."

Former president Jimmy Carter has condemned the prison conditions at Guantanamo Bay.

The unusual legal status of Guantanamo Bay was a factor in the choice of that location as a prison center. The U.S. government claimed that because Gitmo is on Cuban soil, prisoners there do not have the constitutional rights they would otherwise have if they were on U.S. soil. (For example, prisoners can be held without charges brought against them, without legal representation by a lawyer, for an indefinite length of time—all of which would be violations of U.S. civil rights.) However, the Supreme Court rejected this argument in a 2004 case on the grounds that the United States has exclusive control over Guantanamo Bay.

THE PATRIOT ACT

Following the attacks of September 11, 2001, the U.S. Congress passed the USA PATRIOT Act (Uniting and Strengthening America by Providing Appropriate Tools Required to Intercept and Obstruct Terrorism Act of 2001). This act broadened the abilities of U.S. law enforcement agencies to conduct searches, and detain and deport prisoners regarded as potential terrorists. In June 2005, President Bush stated that terrorism investigations under the act have resulted in more than 400 charges, more than half of which resulted in convictions, though in some of these cases, prosecutors chose to charge suspects with non-terror-related crimes such as immigration, fraud, and conspiracy. Critics of the PATRIOT Act have especially objected to "sneak and peak" searches, in which government agents may search a person's home or business without notifying the subject of the search—an action that would otherwise violate citizens' constitutional rights. A 2005 Amnesty International report criticizes the unlawful detainment without charge of several U.S. citizens, another example of civil rights violations conducted under the act.

According to a report released June 27, 2005, by Human Rights Watch and the American Civil Liberties Union, "Operating behind a wall of secrecy, the U.S. Department of Justice thrust scores of Muslim men living in the United States into . . . indefinite detention without charge and baseless accusations of terrorist links." The report documents that the

Since the PATRIOT Act, a Muslim man living in the United States may no longer be protected by the rights of due process.

government detained sixty-nine Muslims shortly after the September 11, 2001, terrorist attacks; the government charged fewer than half of them with a crime and did not inform many of them of the reason for their arrests. Many were not allowed immediate access to a lawyer and were not permitted to see the evidence used against them. According to the report,

> Witnesses were typically arrested at gunpoint, held around the clock in solitary confinement, and subjected to the harsh and degrading high-security conditions usually reserved for prisoners accused or convicted of the most dangerous crimes. Corrections staff verbally harassed the detainees and, in some cases, physically abused them.

As of early July 2005, the U.S. government has not confirmed these allegations.

FREEDOMS VERSUS PUBLIC SAFETY: DIFFICULT ISSUES FOR THE UNITED STATES

Alleged mistreatment of prisoners at Guantanamo Bay and alleged abuses of persons under the PATRIOT Act are problems related to a difficult moral question: At what point should a government violate some people's rights in order to protect others from possible attacks? A popular television drama, the FOX network show *24*, portrayed this dilemma in its 2005 season: there were repeated scenes where counterterrorism agent Jack Bauer tortured prisoners in order to obtain information to prevent a nuclear attack on the United States. Likewise, a 2002 poll by the Gallup organization found that almost half of U.S. citizens interviewed would be willing to give up some of their constitutional freedoms in order to prevent future terrorist attacks.

Critics of the PATRIOT Act compare its premises to that of Adolf Hitler's.

Trading civil rights for security seems logical to some citizens. Isn't it better to jail or torture a few people than to allow many people to suffer from terrorist attacks? However, historians and philosophers caution against thinking that "the ends justify the means," pointing out that the Nazis and Russian communists, noted for human rights abuses, operated on just such assumptions. Harsh treatment of prisoners and unconstitutional invasions of privacy could make the United States safer, but should a nation that has led the world in freedom resort to the same methods it has criticized in other countries? These are difficult questions, and future citizens will have to carefully discuss and act on them.

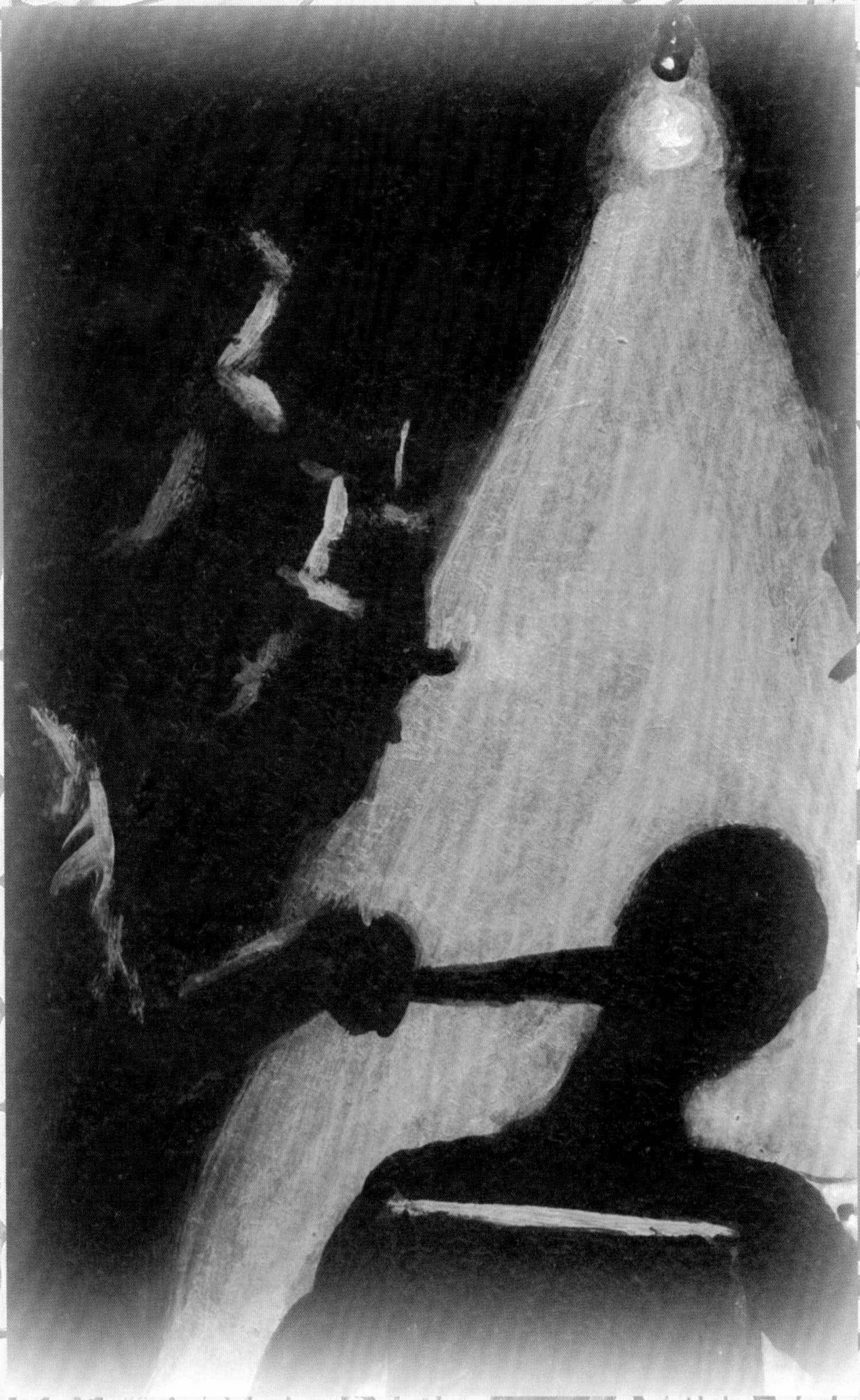

CHAPTER 6

THE STRUGGLE FOR FREEDOM CONTINUES

"Please use your liberty to promote ours."
—political prisoner Aung San Suu Kyi

Dr. Wang Bingzhang is today serving a life sentence in a Chinese jail in Guangdong Province, a punishment for alleged political "crimes" he committed entirely outside of China, and despite the fact that he was not in China when arrested. Dr. Wang was born in China but attained his medical degree in Canada. He worked for decades writing articles and organizing groups to work on behalf of Chinese democracy, all done

Guangdong Province in China, where Wang Bingzhang is imprisoned

"I knew that my case had become public. . . . Then the pressure on me decreased and conditions improved."

—Professor Luiz Rossi of Brazil, explaining how an Amnesty International letter-writing campaign improved his situation as a political prisoner

as a Chinese citizen in exile. He has permanent resident status in the United States, and his sister and daughter are U.S. citizens.

In 2002, Dr. Wang and two companions traveled to Vietnam to meet with supporters of democracy in China. A group of ten men dressed in civilian clothes surrounded the pro-democracy workers and ordered them to come quietly. They placed Dr. Wang in a speedboat and raced to China. As of December 2005, he was held in a Chinese prison despite protests from the United Nations, and his health was poor. In a letter to the media in August 2005, Dr. Wang's son, Times Wang, wrote that his father had suffered two strokes.

Although the Chinese government continues to claim that Wang is a "terrorist," Thai police **exonerated** him in August 2005 of any connection to the plot to bomb the Chinese embassy in Bangkok. This had been the key charge in the Chinese government's charges against Dr. Wang. The Chinese government stands by their charges, and Dr. Wang remains imprisoned. Friends and supporters are adamant that his only crime is that of urging democracy in China. He is one of thousands of men, women, and even a few children, imprisoned in various nations today for political reasons.

THE STUGGLE FOR FREEDOM CONTINUES

China has a much more modern and Western look today than it once did.

ASIA

China has certainly changed in recent years, with a new openness to capitalism, "hip" styles, and innovative artists and inventors coming to the forefront of Chinese society. However, human rights are still a concern, as the kidnapping of Dr. Wang demonstrates. A 2005 Amnesty International report notes that the government often labels political ***dissidents*** or religious figures "terrorists," then imprisons or executes them. There are still reports of prisoners killed for sale of organs. Furthermore, according to Mickey Spiegel, a senior researcher in the Asia Division of

Despite China's legal reforms, Mao Tse-tung's influence can still be felt.

THE STUGGLE FOR FREEDOM CONTINUES

Ethnic minorities in Myanmar have been forced to relocate to government centers.

YOU CAN HELP FREE THEM

Aung San Suu Kyi has asked people around the world, "Please use your liberty to promote ours." Countless men, women, and children around the world today are political prisoners. Working together, staying informed, and using the power of their influence, citizens around the globe can bring freedom to these political prisoners. By taking time to act, *you* can help free them.

Human Rights Watch, "In spite of China's rhetoric about legal reform . . . the Chinese government still does not tolerate uncontrolled political or religious activity." This is true in occupied Tibet as well as mainland China.

Manmar also continues to imprison dissidents. As of July 2005, the Burmese military government incarcerates some 1,300 political rights activists, along with Aung San Suu Kyi. In addition, the Burmese government has forced some half million ethnic minority members to relocate to government-sponsored centers or projects, and there are numerous recent cases of religious persecution as well.

THE MIDDLE EAST

One change in the first years of the twenty-first century is the defeat of Saddam Hussein's Ba'ath Party control over Iraq following U.S. military

Saudi Arabia prides itself on its modern society, but its citizens lack the privilege of free speech.

POLITICAL PRISONER SUPPORT

intervention. Hussein's regime had imprisoned and tortured many political dissidents. While that source of political imprisonment might have been eliminated, that is not the end of the story for political imprisonment in the Middle East. In June 2005, Egypt arrested 800 members of the group Muslim Brotherhood, holding some 300 of those without charge, an example of Egypt's continuing use of imprisonment to stifle political dissent. Iran's government likewise squashes political opposition by political imprisonment, solitary confinement, torture, and trials without *due process.* In Saudi Arabia, "For all its talk of democratic reforms, the Saudi government is imposing long prison terms on those who call for peaceful political change," said Sarah Leah Whitson, executive director of Human Rights Watch's Middle East & North Africa Division, in a May 2005 report. She went on to explain that, "In handing down such

THE STUGGLE FOR FREEDOM CONTINUES

brutal sentences, the Saudi authorities are trampling on the right to free speech."

AFRICA

In June 2005, a disputed election in Ethiopia led to government forces killing hundreds and imprisoning thousands of its citizens who opposed the government. In Sudan, in the context of a continuing civil war, paramilitary groups allied with the government have killed, raped, enslaved, and relocated masses of civilians. On the Ivory Coast, tension between the government and rebel groups has been cause for political killings, massacres, "disappearances," and torture.

AMNESTY INTERNATIONAL AND OTHER ORGANIZATIONS' WORK ON BEHALF OF POLITICAL PRISONERS

You may think, "There are so many political prisoners and so many nations that abuse human rights—what difference can someone like me make in the world?" In fact, individuals can make a difference. Former political prisoners say repeatedly that the actions of people around the world made a difference in their situation. Protests, e-mails, letters, and even prayers from concerned people sustained them and eventually brought about their release.

Several organizations are dedicated to supporting political prisoners. Some organizations, like the Leonard Peltier Defense Committee, commit themselves to one person's cause. Others, like the U.S. Campaign for Burma, focus on prisoners within one nation. Amnesty International is a large international organization dedicated to protecting human rights all over the world. Begun in 1961, Amnesty International now has 1.7 million members in 160 countries. The top goals of the organization are freedom for prisoners of conscience, fair and prompt trials for political prisoners, and an end to the death penalty, torture, and other cruel treatment. Amnesty International conducts campaigns and "urgent actions," requesting letters and faxes to be sent on behalf of specific prisoners. Members write the government of the detainees, urging their release and informing them that people around the world are concerned.

GLOSSARY

apartheid: A political system in South Africa from 1948 until the early 1990s that separated the different peoples living there and gave privileges to those of European origin.

arbitrary: Based solely on personal wishes, feelings, or perceptions, rather than on objective facts.

asylum: Protection from arrest and extradition.

atrocities: Shockingly cruel acts of violence against an enemy in wartime.

boycotts: Refusals to deal with something as a form of protest.

civil rights: Rights that all citizens of a society are supposed to have.

coup: The sudden overthrow of a government and seizure of political power, usually in a violent manner and by the military.

dissidents: Those who publicly disagree with an established political or religious system or organization.

dubious: Of uncertain quality, intention, or appropriateness.

due process: The entitlement of a citizen to proper legal procedures and natural justice.

emaciated: Extremely thin, especially due to starvation or illness.

exonerated: Declared someone is not guilty of a crime.

expunged: Deleted from a written record.

heinous: Shockingly evil or wicked.

KGB: The secret police of the former Soviet Union.

pogram: A planned campaign of persecution or extermination sanctioned by a government and directed against a particular ethnic group, especially in Russia.

stand down: To go off an alert status.

stave off: To hold off; repel.

totalitarian: Relating to or operating a centralized government system in which a single party without opposition rules over political, economic, social, and cultural life.

zealous: Actively enthusiastic.

FURTHER READING

Banks, Deena. *Amnesty International*. Milwaukee, Wis.: World Almanac Library, 2004.

Havel, Vaclav. *Disturbing the Peace*. New York: Vintage Books, 1990.

Jingsheng, Wei. *The Courage to Stand Alone*. New York: Viking, 1997.

Mandela, Nelson. *Mandela: An Illustrated Biography*. New York: Little, Brown and Company, 1996.

Oufkir, Malika. *Stolen Lives: Twenty Years in a Desert Jail*. New York: Hyperion, 1997.

Peltier, Leonard. *Prison Writings: My Life Is a Sun Dance.* New York: Crazy Horse Spirit Inc., 1999.

Suu Kyi, Aung San. *Freedom From Fear and Other Writings*. New York: Viking, 1991.

Wu, Harry. *Troublemaker: One Man's Crusade Against China's Cruelty.* New York: Random House, 1996.

Zana, Leyla. *Writings from Prison*. Watertown, Mass.: Blue Crane, 1999.

FOR MORE INFORMATION

Amnesty International
www.amnesty.org

Daw Aung San Suu Kyi
www.dassk.org/index.php

Freedom Now
www.freedomnow.org

Human Rights Watch
hrw.org

The Leonard Peltier Defense Committee
www.leonardpeltier.org

The Mobilization to Free Mumia Abu-Jamal
www.freemumia.org

The Official Web site of Vaclav Havel
www.vaclavhavel.cz

U.S. Campaign for Burma
www.uscampaignforburm.org

Publisher's note:
The Web sites listed on this page were active at the time of publication.
The publisher is not responsible for Web sites that have changed their
addresses or discontinued operation since the date of publication. The
publisher will review and update the Web-site list upon each reprint.

BIBLIOGRAPHY

Banks, Deena. *Amnesty International*. Milwaukee, Wis.: World Almanac Library, 2004.

Daw Aung San Suu Kyi. http://www.dassk.org/index.php. (Accessed December 28, 2005)

Elie Wiesel. http://xroads.virginia.edu/~CAP/HOLO/ELIEBIO.HTM.

F-18: China Attempts to Control Religious Leadership in Tibet. http://www.forum18.org/Archive.php?article_id=584.

Federation of American Scientists: The Kurds in Turkey. http://www.fas.org/asmp/profiles/turkey_background_kurds.htm.

The Free Leonard Peltier Committee. http://www.leonardpeltier.org. (Accessed December 28, 2005)

Havel, Vaclav. *Disturbing the Peace*. New York: Vintage Books, 1990.

Jingsheng, Wei. *The Courage to Stand Alone*. New York: Viking, 1997.

Justice for Police Officer Daniel Faulkner. http://www.danielfaulkner.com.

Mandela, Nelson. *Mandela: An Illustrated Biography*. New York: Little, Brown and Company, 1996.

The Mobilization to Free Mumia Abu-Jamal. http://www.freemumia.org.

A Nutshell Biography of Mahatma Gandhi. http://ssinha.com/biogandhi.htm.

Oufkir, Malika. *Stolen Lives: Twenty Years in a Desert Jail*. New York: Hyperion, 1997.

Peltier, Leonard. *Prison Writings: My Life is a Sun Dance*. New York: Crazy Horse Spirit Inc., 1999.

REM Protests Burmese Treatment of Aung San Suu Kyi. http://www.soulshine.ca/news/newsarticle.php?nid=2169.

Suu Kyi, Aung San. *Freedom from Fear and Other Writings*. New York: Viking, 1991.

Wu, Harry. *Troublemaker: One Man's Crusade Against China's Cruelty*. New York: Random House, 1996.

Zana, Leyla. *Writings from Prison*. Watertown, Mass.: Blue Crane, 1999.

INDEX

POLITICAL PRISONERS

PICTURE CREDITS

Chapter opening art was taken from a painting titled *The Interrogation* by Raymond Gray.

Raymond Gray has been incarcerated since 1973. Mr. Gray has learned from life, and hard times, and even from love. His artwork reflects all of these.

BIOGRAPHIES

AUTHOR

Roger Smith holds a degree in English education and formerly taught in the Los Angeles public schools. Smith did volunteer work with youthful inmates at a juvenile detention facility in Los Angeles. He currently lives in Arizona.

SERIES CONSULTANT

Dr. Larry E. Sullivan is Associate Dean and Chief Librarian at the John Jay College of Criminal Justice and Professor of Criminal Justice in the doctoral program at the Graduate School and University Center of the City University of New York. He first became involved in the criminal justice system when he worked at the Maryland Penitentiary in Baltimore in the late 1970s. That experience prompted him to write the book *The Prison Reform Movement: Forlorn Hope* (1990; revised edition 2002). His most recent publication is the three-volume *Encyclopedia of Law Enforcement* (2005). He has served on a number of editorial boards, including the *Encyclopedia of Crime and Punishment,* and *Handbook of Transnational Crime and Justice.* At John Jay College, in addition to directing the largest and best criminal justice library in the world, he teaches graduate and doctoral level courses in criminology and corrections. John Jay is the only liberal arts college with a criminal justice focus in the United States. Internationally recognized as a leader in criminal justice education and research, John Jay is also a major training facility for local, state, and federal law enforcement personnel.